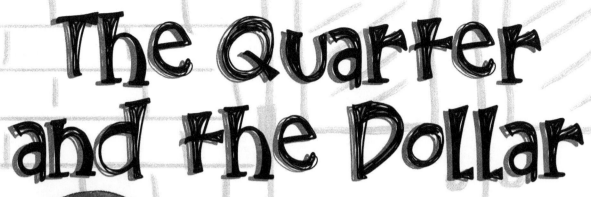

The Quarter and the Dollar

Written by
Stephanie Ann DePalma

Illustrated by
Julia Pelikhovich

Quincy Quarter was a coin,
Silver, smooth, and round.
He had a skinny figure,
And he didn't weigh a pound.

One day when Quincy asked his mom,
"Hey, Mom, what am I worth?"
"A quarter is worth 25 cents
All around the Earth."

Quincy Quarter loved that he was greater than a dime,
Greater than a nickel and a penny both combined!

But then one day when Quincy Quarter had to get to class,
He bumped right into Donnie Dollar walking way too fast.

"Look what we have here," he said;
"It's little Quincy Quarter.
You're probably not even worth
As much as bottled water."

Quincy Quarter thought of this and started to get sad.
What Donnie Dollar said to him made him feel really bad.

He thought that being 25 cents was worth a great amount.
It's 5 away from 30, which is really quick to count.

That night when Quincy made it home, he couldn't even eat. The way that Donnie Dollar made him feel was pure defeat.

He told himself that he would go to school the next day early.
"Maybe he won't see me, and I'll have a great day surely."

So Quincy Quarter went to school
Real early the day after;
And as he quickly walked to class,
He heard the sound of laughter.

10

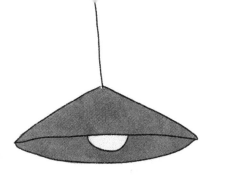
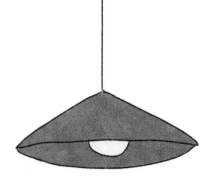

"Hey, Quincy Quarter, you're not even
Worth a piece of gum!"
When Donnie Dollar shouted this,
Quincy became numb.

"You're worthless, Quincy Quarter;
You need four of you to make me.
And if somebody had to choose between us,
They would take me."

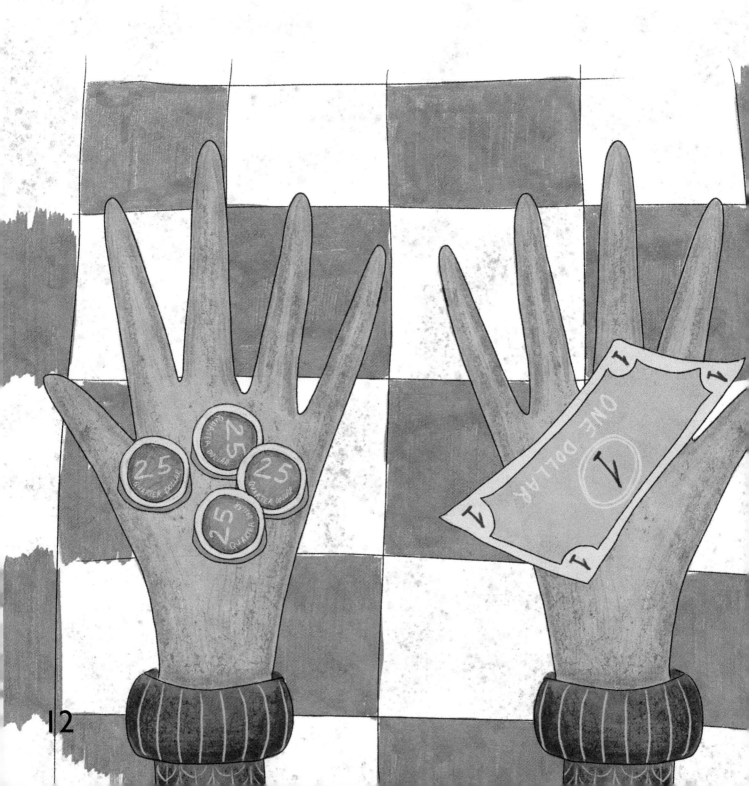

Quincy Quarter couldn't take the teasing any longer.
The weaker he became, Donnie Dollar became stronger.

"Hahahahaha!" laughed the other dollars, mean and grim.
Not even Penny Pam nor Nancy Nickel stuck by him.

14

"Come on," said Donnie Dollar to his other dollar friends; "Let's eat our lunch outside today," he said to all of them.

And as they went outside and played,
Something strange took place.
Water drops began to fall
On Donnie Dollar's face.

And as the droplets turned to rain
And rain turned into flood,
Donnie Dollar soon began
To mush into the mud.

17

And as the other coins got wet and went to run inside,
They stepped all over Donnie Dollar as he yelled and cried.

18

"Help!" said Donnie Dollar to his other dollar friends.
But they had all run back inside to get dried up again.

None of Donnie Dollar's friends came back to make him better. Donnie Dollar had no one to tape him back together.

But out of nowhere came a figure, rolling on the ground.
It looked so smooth and silver, and its face was very round.

"Quincy Quarter, is that you?" Donnie Dollar questioned.
"Yes, it's I," said Quincy Quarter without any aggression.

"Why would you come help me?
All I do is treat you poorly.
I laugh at you and call you names and act so immaturely."

23

Quincy Quarter thought of this, and calmly he replied,
"Forgiving and forgetting makes me feel better inside."

Then Quincy picked up Donnie Dollar
Off the muddy floor,
He threw him right above his head
And brought him through the door.

"Although my value is lower
And this may make me look weak,
You have strengths and I have strengths
That make us both...

26

...UnIQuE."

Look!
Dollar!

He got some tape and put the rips of paper
Back together.
It turned out mending Donnie Dollar's wounds
Made him feel better.

28

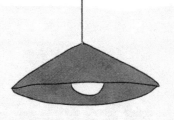

At that moment all the other dollars walked right in.
Quincy Quarter waited for the laughter to begin.

29

Quincy started walking in the opposite direction,
Waiting for the words that made him feel the true rejection.

Until he heard a voice that yelled out, "Quincy, please come here!
Come sit with us in class, and come eat lunch with us all year."

Quincy turned around, and with the biggest smile ever,
He walked towards all the coins and dollars standing all together.

32

"I'm sorry for it all," Donnie Dollar said to Quincy. "I'm thankful and I'm glad that you were able to forgive me." 33

And from that day they ate at lunch and always played together.
The quarter and the dollar had remained best friends forever.

CPSIA information can be obtained
at www.ICGtesting.com
Printed in the USA
BVHW022225180720
584072BV00022B/181